sweet Dreams
Dulces sueños

by Pat Mora

Illustrated by Maribel Suárez

 *An Imprint of HarperCollinsPublishers*

When Grandma comes to tuck us in, she says,
Cuando Abuelita viene a darnos las buenas noches dice:

"Shh, shh, the squirrels are sleeping."

—Shh, shh . . . las ardillas están durmiendo.

And Grandma kisses Danny.
Y Abuelita le da un besito a Danny.

She says, "Shh, shh, the bunnies are sleeping."

Dice —Shh, shh . . . los conejitos están durmiendo.

Grandma kisses Tina.
Abuelita le da un besito a Tina.

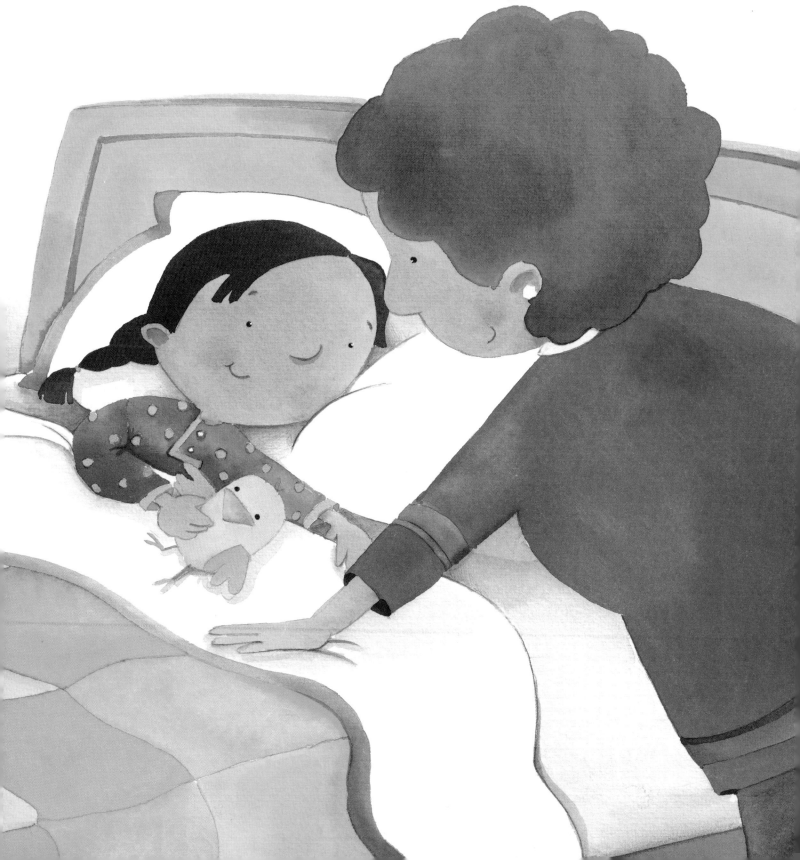

"Shh, shh, the birds are sleeping."

—Shh, shh . . . los pajaritos están durmiendo.

She says, "Shh, shh, the kitten is sleeping."
Dice —Shh, shh . . . la gatita está durmiendo.

"Shh, shh, Tico is sleeping."

—Shh, shh . . . Tico está durmiendo.

"Shh, shh, the stars are shining."
—Shh, shh . . . las estrellas están brillando.

Then Grandma says,
"Shh, shh, the moon is smiling."
Luego, Abuelita dice:
—Shh, shh . . . la luna está sonriendo.

"Shh, shh, your eyes are closing."
—Shh, shh . . . cierra los ojitos . . .

And she kisses me and says,
"Shh, shh, shh, shh, shh, shh."

Y me da un besito y dice:
—Shh, shh, shh, shh, shh, shh . . .

"Sweet dreams."

—Dulces sueños.

To my gentle and supportive editor, Rosemary Brosnan
—P.M.

A Rosemary Brosnan, mi tierna editora,
quien siempre me da su apoyo
—P.M.

Rayo is an imprint of HarperCollins Publishers.

Sweet Dreams / Dulces sueños
Text copyright © 2008 by Pat Mora
Illustrations copyright © 2008 by Maribel Suárez

Manufactured in China.
Library of Congress Cataloging-in-Publication Data is available.
ISBN-13: 978-0-06-085041-8 (trade bdg.) — ISBN-13: 978-0-06-085042-5 (lib. bdg.)

Typography by Stephanie Bart-Horvath
1 2 3 4 5 6 7 8 9 10
❖
First Edition